Ava Imotichey

The Purple People Eater

To order additional copies of this book, contact:
Xlibris
844-714-8691
www.Xlibris.com
Orders@Xlibris.com

ISBN: Softcover   978-1-6641-9578-3
        Hardcover   978-1-6641-9577-6
        EBook   978-1-6641-9579-0

Print information available on the last page

Rev. date: 01/07/2022

The Purple People Eater

This is an old story, first told a long time ago. It was passed down from generation to generation. Then it was simply forgotten. Some people say it is true; some say it is a fairy tale.

general store

mayors office

sheriff

candles

blacksmith

butcher shop

doctor office

Nordicland Town

A long, long time ago, there was a town called Nordicland in northern Minnesota. Most of the residents were Scandinavian. The town had a butcher, a baker, a candlestick maker, a blacksmith, and a doctor. There was a general store, a bank, a school, and a church. The town had a mayor, Mr. Swen Anderson, and a town council. The town also had a sheriff, though there was very little crime. The Europeans who worked in town lived in town. But most of Europeans lived on their farms or ranches outside of town. Some Europeans raised wheat and corn; others raised cattle, horses, chickens, and pigs. Some Europeans worked at the lumber mill by the river.

Several miles away from the town lived the Anishanabe, which translates as "the people." The Europeans them called the Chippewa. They hunted, raised some crops, and grew rice. Some of them lived in town. Some of the Europeans lived with the Anishanabe. There was a great deal of trading between the two groups. The chief of Anishanabe, White Feather, encouraged his people to interact with the Europeans. For the most part, they all got along. There were some Anishanabe and some Europeans who did not trust one another. Those people had ancestors or friends who had been injured or killed by the other side.

Both the Anishanabe and the Europeans participated in the other group's activities. Many of the Anishanabe would attend birthday parties, weddings, and festivals, and some attended church. Many of the Europeans took part in the celebrations of the Anishanabe. Some of the Anishanabe would intermarry with the Europeans. Some couples chose to live in town or on their ranches or farms. Some couples chose to live with the Anishanabe. As a result, there were children who had a mixed heritage. The Anishanabe shared their culture—including language, medicine, proper care of nature, songs, and stories—with the Europeans. The Europeans shared their knowledge of medicine, language, songs, and stories. Most of the Anishanabe and the Europeans respected each other.

The Europeans told a story about a Purple People Eater. He lived in a cave deep in the woods of what is now Minnesota. He had one bulging red eye, a long, wart-covered nose, and a mouth filled with sharp black teeth. Strings of dark drool came out of his mouth. He was covered with long, matted purple hair and had huge hairy arms. His fingers and toes had black nails. He hated water, so he smelled horrible. He only came out when people were angry and fearful. His favorite food was angry, fearful people. He hated love, peace, hope, respect, and friendship. If there were only a few people who were angry, he did not bother.

He only came out when a lot of people were angry and fearful. The way to keep the Purple People Eater away was to practice peace, love, and harmony.

Chief White Feather had a son named Bright Star. Bright Star wanted to work at the sawmill. He hoped to marry Sara Anderson, Swen and Hilda Anderson's daughter, and he needed to earn money to build a house for his future wife.

Bright Star was hired at the sawmill, and he was a good worker. Even though he was the only Anishanabe working at the sawmill, most of the other workers accepted him. Except for Jon White—some of his relatives had been killed by "Injuns."

He grumbled about not trusting "Injuns." Most people just ignored him or politely told him to be quiet. Jon still did not trust Bright Star. Bright Star tried to stay away from Jon.

One day one of the sawmill workers, George Johnson, and Bright Star were walking along the edge of a cliff along the river. George tripped and fell over the edge of the cliff. Bright Star tried to catch him but could not. George fell, broke his neck, and died.

Jon White saw this happen and then told everyone Bright Star pushed George. Bright Star said he was trying to help George. At first, most people believed Bright Star. But Jon White kept insisting that Bright Star pushed the other man

Little by little, people started avoiding the Anishanabe. Soon the Anishanabe were not welcome in town. The Europeans who lived with the tribe were not welcome to stay. There was a lot of fear and anger among both the Anishanabe and the Europeans.

Deep in the cave in the woods, the Purple People Eater woke up. He sniffed and sniffed. He smelled his favorite things: fear and anger, quite a lot of both. His purple hair was all matted and dirty. He yawned, and long, gooey black strings of drool came out of his mouth. He stretched his big, hairy arms and his hands, with their dirty, jagged fingernails. He stretched his legs and feet, with their dirty, jagged toenails. Then he slowly started walking toward the source of the smell of fear and anger.

That day, Little River of the Anishanabe tribe was hunting deer deep in the woods. He spotted the Purple People Eater slowly lumbering toward town and ran back to tell the tribe. To his dismay, no one believed him. Little River had actually left the deer he shot behind when he saw the Purple People Eater, so Big Bear went back to get the deer. Then he saw the Purple People Eater lumbering slowly along toward town. Big Bear ran back to the tribe to tell them what he saw.

Chief White Feather called a council of elders to discuss the situation.

There was a problem. But the Europeans no longer welcomed the Anishanabe in their town, so they could not warn them. However, they knew the Purple People Eater would be coming to the tribe because of the fear and anger within the tribe. The Anishanabe had to rid themselves of the fear and anger. They started praying and singing and dancing.

Peter Smith, one of the Europeans, went out hunting and saw the Purple People Eater. He could not believe his eyes and thought, *There really is such a creature?* He went back to tell the townspeople, who laughed at him. But Jim Swanson decided to take a look. Sure enough—there was the ugliest creature he had ever seen.

Jim went back to town and insisted on calling a town council meeting. So all the townspeople, ranchers, and farmers met. They discussed the creature and what to do about it. After hours of talking, they decided to try to meet with the Anishanabe.

They sent the Mayor Swen Anderson and one of the councilmen, Mr. John Bergman.

The two men were surprised when the Anishanabe greeted them warmly. The men and the people of the tribe talked for many hours. They agreed the incident that started the trouble was the accident at the cliff. Mr. Anderson and Mr. Bergman said they were authorized by the town council to negotiate any settlement that was agreed upon. They agreed to accept that what happened at the cliff was an accident and no one was to blame. They agreed that the Anishanabe would be welcome in town and could start trading again.

Mr. Anderson and Mr. Bergman took this agreement to the town council and all the townspeople.

The Europeans decided to have a big festival with singing and dancing. The Europeans welcomed the Anishanabe back to town, and the Anishanabe welcomed the Europeans back to the tribe.

There was a huge sigh of relief on both sides. The conflict had made everyone nervous and edgy. Now they could relax. Jon White never apologized, but he never said another word against the Anishanabe again.

Bright Star continued to work for the sawmill and was able to build a house.

Bright Star and Sara Anderson had a wonderful wedding, and everyone celebrated together. There was peace and tranquility all around.

In the woods, the Purple People Eater stopped and sniffed and sniffed. He did not smell the fear and anger anymore. He just sighed, shrugged his dirty shoulders, turned around, and shuffled back to his nice dark, dirty cave.

Printed in the United States
by Baker & Taylor Publisher Services